Stand Down

Also by J. A. Jance

Joanna Brady Mysteries

J. P. Beaumont Mysteries

Stand Down

A J. P. BEAUMONT NOVELLA

J. A. JANCE

WITNESS
IMPULSE
An Imprint of HarperCollinsPublishers

Excerpt from *Dance of the Bones* copyright © 2015 by J. A. Jance.

EPub Edition MAY 2015 ISBN: 9780062418487
Print Edition ISBN: 9780062418494

10 9 8 7 6 5 4 3 2 1

For Audrey and Celeste

As THE MACHINE spat out the last drops of coffee that Monday morning, a tiny whiff of hairspray wafted down the hallway from Mel's bathroom and mingled with the aroma of freshly ground beans and the distinctive fragrance of Hoppe's #9 gun-cleaning solvent. While she was down the hall getting ready to go to work, I was in the kitchen cleaning our weapons—her standard-issue Smith & Wesson and her backup Glock, along with my own Glock as well.

It's what I did these Monday mornings—clean our weapons—while she got ready to go to work in Bellingham and while I got ready to do whatever it is I do these days. I don't suppose the architect who designed our penthouse condo imagined that our granite countertop would often double as a gun-cleaning workshop, but then again, where else would I do this necessary, lifesaving task—the living room? It only takes once to learn how completely a tiny piece of pistol innards can disappear into the hidden reaches of a plush living-room carpet. And cleaning her weapons every Monday morning was my small contribution toward keeping her safe.

The hairspray told me that within a minute or so, my wife, Mel, would emerge from her bathroom dressed, made up, properly coiffed, and ready to go out into the world as the city of Bellingham's newly hired police chief.

While I was married to my first wife, Karen, we'd shared a single bathroom, with a single washbasin and a combination tub and shower. By the time Anne Corley, my second wife, came into my life, however briefly, I still had a single bathroom, but it contained two washbasins, and a tub/shower combo. Shortly after Mel Soames and I tied the knot, it became clear that even a deluxe bathroom, one with two basins, a tub, and a stand-alone shower, simply wouldn't cut it.

Mel had solved the problem by collecting her lotions and potions and decamping to the far end of the hallway and turning the guest bedroom, bathroom, and closet into her private domain. At the time, since we were both working the same shifts for the same outfit, having separate bathrooms worked for us. Now things had changed. She had a relatively new job. As for me? I was struggling with the uncomfortable realities of being newly and quite unwillingly retired.

Mel came down the hall, looking very official in her spiffy police chief's uniform and a pair of sensible, low-heeled pumps.

"Good morning, gorgeous," I told her. I knew she had a meeting with the Bellingham mayor, the city manager, and city council that morning, and I also knew she was dreading it. "Girls in uniform always turn me on."

She stopped and glared at me. "Don't lie," she said. "You know I look like hell."

The truth is, and much to my surprise, she did look like hell. There were dark shadows under her eyes that even deftly applied makeup didn't quite cover. I had spent the night lying next to her in bed as she had tossed and turned her way through the hours. During my years in law enforcement, including twenty or so at Seattle P.D., I had never once entertained the idea of climbing the treacherous career ladder from being an ordinary cop to becoming one of the brass. Mel was different. She had been on the cop-to-brass path in a previous jurisdiction when those plans had been derailed by a complicated divorce. That detour had brought her to Washington State, where we had met.

Second chances don't come along all that often. This time one had. Earlier the previous fall, Mel had been offered her dream job as chief of police in Bellingham, Washington, a small city some ninety miles north of Seattle. The moment the job was offered, I knew she wanted to take it, so I supported her in that decision. I had, however, tried to warn her that making the transition from being part of a team of investigators to being top dog in a new department wouldn't be an easy one. It turns out I was right.

Previously, Mel and I had both worked for the Washington State Attorney General, Ross Connors, on his Special Homicide Investigation Team or, as we had been perversely proud to call it, the S.H.I.T. squad. Ross had been the best boss either of us ever had, bar none. He had expected his people to deliver excellent results while, at the same time, giving his teams of investigators an amazing amount of autonomy. Ross was a political animal, but politics stopped at the door to his office.

I knew even before Mel sat down at her desk that she would find herself in a political quagmire and probably with a dearth of support from the rank and file. Unfortunately, that was proving to be the case. Mel's second-in-command, Assistant Chief Austin Manson, evidently thought the chief's job should have been his for the asking, and he hadn't been happy when she was chosen over him. From what she'd said, I had gleaned that Manson was a much-divorced kind of guy with a rancorous and still-ongoing child-custody battle in his background, along with a few anger-management issues besides. Mel had spent the whole weekend distant and preoccupied. I suspected Manson was the root of the problem, but she hadn't been willing to discuss it. I hadn't brought it up, and neither had she.

Now, even without being Mirandized, I understood that in this dicey situation, anything I said could and would be held against me. Besides, handing out a dose of "I told you so," bright and early in the morning, is never a good way to start a new day or week. I couldn't come right out and tell Mel that she should just bust Austin Manson back to the gang and get it over with. And I sure as hell didn't see myself in the role of Sir Galahad, riding in on my white charger to intervene on her behalf, so that morning, I took the line of least resistance.

"Coffee's ready," I said noncommittally, shoving her newly cleaned weapons across the counter. Once she had stowed them in their appropriate holsters, I handed over Mel's favorite mug, loaded with fresh coffee. "This should do the trick."

Mel gave me the benefit of a small, rueful smile. "Thanks," she said, taking a tentative sip. "Coffee is just what the doctor ordered."

That hint of a smile was enough to make me hope that, as far as dealing with women is concerned, maybe I was getting older and wiser.

"What's on your agenda today?" she asked. She had left piles of unfinished paperwork on the dining-room table before we'd gone to bed the night before. She gathered it into a single stack and shoved it into an open briefcase. The stack was bulky enough that closing the case was a bit of a struggle.

"Late this morning, I'm scheduled to drive up to Arlington to meet with the contractor and take a look at the final estimate."

Two and a half months into her new job, Mel was still spending four nights a week at a dreary Execu-Stay Hotel in Bellingham. Once she accepted the job, we had decided that, although we didn't want to give up our penthouse in downtown Seattle, we'd find someplace nearer to her workplace as a second home. As spouse-in-chief, I had been tasked with finding us suitable digs in the Bellingham area that would allow us to stay there when she was working and come and go from Seattle as often as we wished.

Initially, Mel had voted for another condo. I was looking for something else. After decades of high-rise living, I was ready for a pied-à-terre with ... well ... a little actual terre. I wanted a covered patio where, rain or shine, I could walk outside and barbecue steaks for dinner without messing up the kitchen. I also wanted a place where, if the grandkids came to visit, we could put up a volleyball net or fly model airplanes.

My first few meetings with Helen Tate, the Realtor, hadn't gone well. She had evidently checked up on the value of our home in Seattle on the Web, and I could see the dollar signs swimming in her eyes the first time she showed up to take me looking at properties. She had been somewhat dismayed when I fell in love with a vintage-but-dilapidated three-bedroom midcentury modern. Located in the Bayside area of Fairhaven, with a spectacular, cliffside view, it was listed as a "fixer-upper." With plenty of sixty-year-old plumbing issues, lots of dry rot, and a sagging roof, not to mention a collection of more recent but steamy dual-paned windows that had long since lost their seals, the place should have been listed as a tear-down. There was only one problem with that—I wanted it.

The original owner, a widower, had recently been carted off to an Alzheimer's' facility. His son, who lived out of state, simply wanted to dispose of the place with the least possible amount of effort and fuss.

The thing is, I could tell that underneath all the filth and trash, the house had good bones. The spectacular view of the bay, the interior courtyard, and the expansive windows all beckoned to me. There was so much glass that, once the fogged windows were replaced, we'd be able to see right through the house from back to front.

You can get those kinds of views in high-rise condos occasionally, but finding them in a house was unusual.

Even so, I hoped it would be possible for Mel to see past the neglect to the house's buried charm. Something about the old place felt familiar and inviting and made me want to bring the derelict back from the dead. That stormy day in February, when Mel agreed to meet Helen and me at the house during her lunch break, both the Realtor and I held our collective breaths as Mel, dressed in her uniform and heels, wandered thoughtfully from room to room.

"I see what you mean," Mel said at last, picking her way through yet another minefield of debris as she returned to the living room. "The place does have good bones, but it's going to take a lot of work. Are you sure you're up to it?"

I nodded.

"What happens to all this stuff?" Mel asked, gesturing at the piles of junk surrounding her.

"The owner's son lives out of town. He doesn't want any of it, and he doesn't want to have to deal with it, either," Helen explained. "He's ready to be done with it."

"We'd be buying the place as is, contents and all, no contingencies," I added. "That means whatever is left here, we'd have to haul away, and whatever's broken, we'd have to fix. I've already called Jim Hunt to see if he'd be willing to come take a look and give us some suggestions."

Mel eyed me speculatively. "Jim Hunt, as in the guy who designed both your bachelor pads?"

I nodded, guilty as charged. After Karen divorced me,

I had moved into a unit at the Royal Crest in downtown Seattle with little more than the clothes on my back and the one piece of furniture that Karen had allowed me to take—my recliner. One of the secretaries at the department had referred me to Jim, and he had done a complete job of creating a livable condo from a barren shell, up to and including linens and pots and pans. Our only disagreement was over the recliner. He wanted it gone, but I was adamant. The recliner was mine, and I was keeping it. In the years since it had been recovered more than once.

Mel wandered over to the spot where a baby grand piano peeked out from under a mountain of magazines and newspapers. "You say everything stays, even this?" she asked, pausing long enough to open the dust-laden lid and play a scale. Even I could hear that the piano was hopelessly out of tune.

Helen nodded. "That, too," the Realtor said helpfully.

"All right, then," Mel said. "I'm headed back to work. As long as the piano is included, you've got my go-ahead to make an offer. When you talk to Jim, see if he knows of a good piano guy who could haul this poor old thing out of here, refinish it, and tune it up. Obviously, it can't stay here if the place is about to turn into a construction zone."

Talk about an assumed close! I learned all about those back in my youth, when I was selling Fuller Brush to earn my way through school. We were trained not to say, "Do you want this brush?" but, rather, "How do you want to pay for this, cash or check?" That was long enough ago that credit cards still weren't an option. It was also typical behavior for Mel Soames. When I asked her to marry me, she hadn't come right out, and said, "Yes." Instead, her response had been more on the order of, "Well, okay. When?"

I don't think that was the reaction the Realtor expected. She was still standing in an openmouthed daze, as Mel walked out of the house, closing the door behind her.

"You're buying it, then?" Helen asked. "Just like that?"

"It's looking good."

I waited for Jim to arrive before making a formal offer. He's a tall, good-looking, narrow guy—maybe even skinny. He's about my age but fared better in the knee lottery than I did since his are still original equipment. He has an enviable head of silvery hair combined with the good looks of an aging movie star. He's also gay and attempting to cut down on his smoking, but in the thirty years we've known one another, neither of those issues—smoking or sexual orientation—have impacted our friendship. He goes his way; I go mine. And he thinks Mel is terrific.

Jim showed up a while later in his shiny white Mercedes C230 and spent the better part of two hours prowling the place before rendering his verdict. "I think we could make do with this," he told me, "but, if you want my help, there's one condition."

"What's that?" I asked.

"The only way I'm tackling this job is if you agree to get rid of that damned recliner. Finally."

When I called Mel to report Jim's single demand, she had jumped at it.

"If he can get you to let go of that ugly old thing, then make an offer on the house and tell me where to sign. I'm there."

And so we did. Once the deal was finalized, the former owner's son and a grandson had dropped by long enough to gather up several boxes of clothing and a few mementoes, then they drove away without so much as a backward glance, leaving behind seven decades' worth of accumulated trash and a houseful of dead and dying furniture and mountains of out-of-date foodstuffs. Some of the canned goods had exploded, leaving behind the distinctive aroma of decay, which would only disappear once we'd stripped the wallboard down to the studs.

That's what we were working on now—the reno. The trash had been hauled away. The piano had been collected by a piano restorer and carted off to be refinished, tuned, and stored until it was safe to come back home.

Originally, the house had been insulated with layers of cedar shavings that, over time, had been reduced to little more than dust. After evicting a family of raccoons that had taken up residence in the attic, we vacuumed out the smelly remains. With that gone, along with the reeking wallboard, the place smelled almost civilized. Jim had come up with an elegant redesign. By sacrificing the third bedroom, he was able to give Mel and me a master bedroom suite that included two separate bathrooms and two walk-in closets.

The master-bedroom plans alone were enough to send Mel over the top with delight, but after that, the project seemed to have stalled out. The challenge now was nailing down a busy contractor and getting him to commit to doing the job in a timely fashion. That was what I was hoping to accomplish today. Only then would we be able to apply for permits and start actual construction.

"I know about the meeting with Jim and that contractor later today," Mel said with a frown, "but aren't you also scheduled to see Harry? He's due to be released from rehab anytime now, isn't he?"

Making Harry I. Ball's house wheelchair accessible was currently my other pressing home-remodeling issue. While waiting for the project in Bellingham to get under way, I—along with Jim's help—had been running point on the renovations to bring Harry I. Ball's house into compliance with his current wheelchair-bound status. His project, too, had been plagued with delays. Now, even though we were down to finishing touches, they all had to be completed, inspected, and signed off on before Harry could be released from rehab to go home.

I nodded. "The foreman told me yesterday that they expect to be done by the end of this week. That's the goal, anyway."

"And you've got Marge lined up to look after him once he's back home?"

Marge Herndon was the crusty retired RN Mel and I had first encountered when I'd hired her to come look after me after my bilateral knee-replacement surgery. The woman was about as warm and fuzzy as a Marine Corps drill sergeant, but she knew how to get the job done, and she had kept me on the straight and narrow as far as rehab was concerned. Harry Ignatius Ball, aka Harry

I. Ball, was a tough customer under the best of circumstances. Now, stuck in a wheelchair, with both legs amputated above the knee, I knew he would be a demanding and difficult patient.

"She's willing," I answered. "She's supposed to show up this morning to meet him for the first time, then we'll see what happens. If those two lock horns, it could turn into World War III."

Standing with one foot out the door, Mel turned back long enough to give me a genuine grin. "I'd love to be a mouse in the corner when that happens. Between Harry I. Ball and Marge Herndon, my money's on Marge—all the way. She managed you just fine, and I'm betting she'll be able to handle him, too. Harry won't know what hit him."

"Drive carefully," I warned her, giving her a goodbye peck on the cheek. "It rained hard overnight. They're saying to watch out for standing water on the roadways."

While Mel took the long elevator ride from our aerie down to the parking garage far below and drove up four sets of ramps to street level, I went out on the balcony and stood waiting for her to emerge. If Mel had known that I did that every morning, rain or shine, when she left for work, she would have thought I was being a sentimental fool, but I couldn't help myself. Now I knew how it felt to be the spouse of a cop heading out the door for a day of confronting the bad guys. For the first time in my life, I understood what it meant to be the one waiting at home, knowing that my beloved would be at work some ninety-one miles and at least two hours away in good traffic.

More if anything went wrong along the way. Yes, karma is definitely a bitch!

So is change.

I walked back inside and made myself another cup of coffee. Then I sat down on the living-room window seat and looked out at the Space Needle. That iconic piece of Seattle's skyline has taken on a whole new and much darker meaning these days. It was where all of our lives had taken a sudden turn in a new and unexpected direction.

THINGS HAD STARTED going haywire almost three months earlier, on the Friday, two weeks before Christmas. Mel was back in her bathroom getting ready for our evening out while I sat in this same window-seat perch looking at the red and green lights, including the glowing Christmas tree that topped the Needle's flying-saucer-shaped roof. Ross Connors had scored the Needle's lower level for a Special Homicide Investigation Team Christmas party. If Ross had been using state funds for the event, he probably would have had to call it a "Holiday Party," but since he was paying for the whole thing out of his own pocket, he would, as he told me, call it whatever the hell he wanted.

The people from all three S.H.I.T. squads—the ones in Spokane and Olympia as well as our Seattle-based one—along with their spouses/partners were invited. Ross was also springing for hotel rooms where necessary. We all knew what the real deal was. It was really a thinly disguised post-election celebration. When the polls had closed the previous November, and when all the votes were counted, Ross Connors had won again despite all the predictions to the contrary. He was still the Attorney General because countless people had crossed party lines to vote for him. The problem was, Ross was the exception. All the other statewide office holders, including the governor himself, now belonged on the "opposite side of the aisle." I hadn't a doubt in my mind that Ross's Christmas party was a poke in the nose at all those folks—a way of letting them know that he was the last man standing.

As for his people, those of us privileged to call Ross Connors "boss"? We really were "his people." Ross had used that same considerable political savvy that had won cross-party-line voters in creating S.H.I.T. He had collected a diverse set of people—always the ones he thought most skilled in getting the job done—and had molded us into a cohesive whole, a team in every sense of the word. If this was a Christmas party, we were all going, and that included the two guys in the organization who describe themselves as "non-observant" Jews.

The event was due to start promptly at six. It was five fifty-five when Mel emerged from her private domain at the far end of the hall. Dressed in a long, ruby-red dress with her long blond hair swept up onto her head, she would have been at home on any Hollywood red carpet. So would the shoes—amazing bright red stiletto heels made by a guy named Jimmy something. They matched her dress perfectly. In four-inch heels, she was only slightly shorter than me. In honor of the evening, she was carrying a small, glittery clutch rather than one of her more customary suitcase-sized purses.

I had sat there, waiting for her and holding her coat. Standing up, I slipped it over her shoulders and inhaled a hint of perfume.

"It's spitting snow," I said. "How about if we take the car and use the valet?"

"Come on," she said. "It's only three blocks."

The thing is, I was well acquainted with almost every inch of those three blocks. Doing rehab in the aftermath of my knee-replacement surgery, I had done more walking than ever before, trudging alone through Seattle's Denny Regrade neighborhood. I knew full well that the Space Needle was a mere three blocks away from Belltown Terrace's front door, but I also understood that those three blocks are lined with mature trees whose roots have, over time, played havoc with nearby sidewalk surfaces. Not only is the concrete lumpy and bumpy in spots, it's also riddled with cracks and iron drain covers that are the natural enemy of misplaced feet, especially ones in very high heels.

"Besides," Mel said, "it'll be fun, and I promise to hold on to your arm for dear life."

"Right," I said, "as in the blind leading the blind."

Someone once told me, "Happy wife; happy life," so we walked, laughing and talking through spattering snow that we both knew would never stick. We crossed Broad at Second then walked up the north side of the street as far as Denny, which we crossed at the light.

Walking along the grassy berm between Denny and

the Pacific Science Center, we were almost at the valet parking entrance at the bottom of the Space Needle and the Chihuly Glass Garden when I heard the first hint of sirens—lots of sirens.

When you live downtown, you grow accustomed to sirens. You learn to differentiate between those of the fire engines and aid cars at the Seattle F.D. station over on Fourth. There are the short bursts from patrol cars that usually indicate traffic stops. Those are especially annoying in the wee hours of the morning, just after the bars let out, when the traffic guys are busy taking drunks off the street. But this was different. This was something more. It sounded like a car chase to me, coming southbound toward us along Elliott. Suddenly, sirens blossomed all around us as police vehicles from all over the city converged on the area. There were cars coming northbound on the avenues from downtown and cars coming down from Queen Anne Hill.

Car chases are inherently dangerous. The potential for tragedy—for death and serious injury—is always there, whether it's on a deserted highway in the middle of the night or on a city street in broad daylight. A car chase during rush hour on a dark and rain-slick city street was insanity itself. Someone else must have come to that same conclusion. The sirens went silent, and I surmised that orders to break off the chase must have been given. The cops got the message. They backed off, all of them. Unfortunately, the crooks didn't.

Let's just say that guys who set out to make a living by robbing banks usually aren't the sharpest pencils in the box. The only place smart bank robbers show up is on scripted television shows. And bank robbers who would pull off a heist in Ballard then head into the city center in rush-hour traffic, hoping to make good their escape, exhibit a particularly astounding brand of stupidity. But that's what these two dimwits had done. They had somehow convinced themselves that if they just made it into the downtown core, they'd be able to blend into traffic and disappear.

In the old days, bank tellers would slip dye packs into the crooks' tote bags that would stain the robber and render the money unusable. These days, tellers have access to packets of bills that come pre-equipped with GPS locator chips. All the teller has to do is activate the chip before slipping it into the bag, and voila. That money is invisibly findable with no car chases necessary. I'm sure that's one of the reasons the chase was called off. The chip was working. The good guys had all the time in the world to track the bad guys down.

So far the two boneheads hadn't figured that out. I heard the squeal of tires behind us as they came screaming up past Western and onto Denny. Then, to my amazement, a set of headlights weaving in and out of oncoming traffic, turned off Denny and onto Broad with other drivers slamming up onto sidewalks in desperate attempts to escape harm. Obviously, the maniac behind the wheel hadn't gotten the memo that Broad is no longer a through street.

Instinctively, Mel and I both headed for higher ground although Mel didn't start up the grassy berm until after

she'd pulled off those damned shoes. We were standing side by side when the robbers flew past us, herding
their stolen Range Rover between rows of stopped cars
and tearing off mirrors and door panels as they went. The
Range Rover slewed sideways directly in front of us then
accelerated up Broad.

I knew what was going to happen long before it did. A
vehicle turned off Fourth. The then, with oncoming traffic apparently stalled, the unsuspecting driver made the
left-hand turn into the Space Needle's valet parking area.
The speeding Range Rover, driving in the wrong lane,
smashed into them midturn, T-boning them, hard.

You can go to movie theaters and watch all the
computer-generated mayhem you want, but none of that
compares to the real thing—to the terrible crash followed by the sickening, grinding sound of twisting metal
coming to rest. And then, out of the sudden silence that
followed the carnage came the haunting sound of not one
but two wailing car horns. They sounded like sentinels
announcing the end of the world, or at least the end of the
world as we knew it.

By then, Mel and I were both moving, toward the
action rather than away from it. There would be other
cops in the neighborhood soon, but we were closer than
anyone else, and in what would soon turn into a massive traffic jam, we'd get there before anyone else could,
too. If the crooks, whose car was closer, managed to exit
their vehicle and tried to take off on foot, we'd be able to
restrain them.

Not surprisingly, neither of them—dumb and dumber—
had been smart enough to wear a seat belt. They had both
been ejected from the vehicle. We found them lying on opposite sides of Broad. I located the first one on the north side
of the street, lying with his head cracked open like a broken
watermelon on the sharp edge of the curb. I didn't need to
check for a pulse to know he was a goner.

The other guy, the passenger, had slammed full-tilt
into a metal utility vault on the far side of the street. Mel
reached him at the same time several passersby did. She
knelt briefly and dropped out of sight. When she straight-
ened up, she caught my eye and gave me the thumbs-
down. So that one was dead, too—no great loss there.
Subsequent computer-generated reconstructions of the
collision estimated that the two dunces were doing seventy and still accelerating when they slammed into the
turning vehicle. There was no sign that the driver ever
touched the brakes.

Knowing those guys were dead, Mel and I turned our
attention toward the other damaged vehicle. It was only
then that we realized, with growing horror, that what we
were seeing, stalled in the middle of Broad, were the still-
smoking remains of Ross Connors's Lincoln Town Car.

Even months later, recalling that horrific scene that
changed all our lives was enough to shock me back to real
time. I set down my coffee mug and headed for the shower.
An hour or so later, when I left Belltown Terrace, I turned
right on Second and drove all the way down to Olive and
used that to make my way up to Harry's rehab facility on

the far side of Capitol Hill. That's the official name for that particular neighborhood, but due to all the hospitals based there, locals generally refer to it as Pill Hill.

In the old days I would have turned right on Broad and over to Fifth to make that trip. Not anymore. For one thing, the city's traffic engineers have fixed it so Broad no longer goes anywhere useful. Besides, I avoid Denny and Broad as much as possible. That's where the accident happened. It's where Ross Connors and his driver, Bill Spade, lost their lives, and it's also where Harry Ignatius Ball lost both his legs.

Just glancing up either of those streets is enough to bring back vivid memories of that nightmarish scene. Ross's aging Lincoln Town Car had been hit so hard that both people on the driver's side of the car—Bill at the wheel and Ross seated directly behind him—had died on impact, crushed to death when the stolen Range Rover plowed into the passenger compartment, ending up with the Rover's front bumper crushed up against the Town-Car's drive shaft.

Momentum from the collision carried the two conjoined vehicles into a nearby light pole with enough force that the pole toppled over. It landed on the roofs of both cars, crumpling metal like so much tissue paper and sending a jagged edge of roof into Harry's lower thighs, nearly severing his legs. The weight of the pole on top of the roof was the only thing that kept him from bleeding to death on the spot.

I had reached in through the wreckage and checked both Bill and Ross. Neither of them had a pulse. They were gone. By then, Mel was on the far side of the car, reaching in through the shattered passenger window and trying to comfort Harry, who was howling in pain. Looking at his legs, I was sure he was a goner, too.

The nearest fire station, at Fourth and Battery, was only five blocks away, but in the sudden snarl of stalled traffic, it could just as well have been in Timbuktu. It seemed to take forever for them to get there with the jaws of life. In fact, an EMT, a young woman, jogging from the station and carrying a first-aid kit, arrived long before anyone else or any other equipment. She was small enough to maneuver inside the tiny space left in the vehicle and somehow managed to fasten two tourniquets around Harry's upper thighs, thus saving his life but dooming his legs. In the meantime, I was left with nothing to do but wish I could slam my fist through someone's face, preferably that of the stupid driver, who was already dead.

Mel and I had set out for the Space Needle just minutes before the party was scheduled to start. It turned out that Ross, too, had been making an uncharacteristically late entrance. I found out later that Harry's car had developed a fuel-pump issue on his way into the city from Bellevue. When he'd called Ross to let him know he'd be late, Ross had insisted that he and Bill drive over Lake Washington on the I-90 bridge, pick Harry up, and bring him to the party. I've always been struck by that old saying about no good deed going unpunished, but having Ross and Bill dead because they'd done nothing more than give Harry a ride was too much.

The jaws of life were not yet on the scene when I realized that if most of the other partygoers were already upstairs, I was the one who would have to deliver the bad news. And so I did, pushing my way into the Space Needle lobby and through the line of holiday revelers waiting for the elevator. People protested vigorously as I fought my way to the head of the line and flashed my badge in front of the boyish-faced operator.

"Skyline Banquet level," I snarled at him. "Now!"

Without a word, he allowed me into the elevator, barred the other waiting passengers by means of a velvet-covered rope, closed the door on them, and pushed the buttons. We rode up in utter silence. "Wait here," I ordered. "I'll be coming right back down."

Just inside the door stood a waiter holding a tray of glasses filled with bubbling champagne. I was tempted to grab one of them. In fact, I was tempted to grab them all and swill them down one after another. Instead, I stopped short and scanned the room.

It took a moment for me to locate Katie Dunn, Ross's secretary. She was talking to Barbara Galvin, Harry's secretary and the cornerstone for Unit B of Special Homicide. Finding both women together was a stroke of luck. Katie must have caught sight of the look on my face. She turned away from Barbara and hurried toward me, with Barbara, also sensing something amiss, close on her heels.

"Beau," Katie asked, frowning, "whatever's the matter?"

With no time to lessen the blow, I blurted it out at once. "There's been a car accident down on the street. Ross is dead, and so's his driver. Harry may not make it, either."

Katie's face drained of all color. "Oh, no!" she whispered. "Ross is dead?"

I nodded. Without a word, Barbara sprinted for the elevator.

"Go with Barbara," Katie said to me. "I'll hold the fort here. Keep me posted."

When I entered the elevator, Barbara was already there, white-faced and furious, screeching into the operator's face. "Go, damn it! What on earth are you waiting for? Go now!"

But I had made a believer of the poor guy. He waited until I stepped on board before pushing the DOWN button. By the time we hit the ground level, Barbara was out of her sequined heels. Holding them in one hand and a tiny beaded clutch in the other, she sprinted out of the elevator and left me in the dust as she pushed through the crush of people waiting for the long-delayed elevator.

I caught up with Barbara only because she was stopped short by a uniformed cop trying to maintain a perimeter around the crash site. "She's with me," I told him, holding up my badge. "Let her through."

We reached the wreckage while firefighters were still maneuvering the jaws of life into position. Despite protests from more than one first responder, Barbara shoved Mel out of the way. "Don't you die on me, you bastard!" she yelled at Harry, snatching his hand from Mel's. Bad as things were, Harry focused his eyes on Barbara's face and favored her with a tiny grin.

"Do my best," he whispered. "I'll do my best."

Believe me, the relationship between Harry I. Ball and

the reformed punk rocker, Barbara Galvin, had nothing to do with an office romance. It was more like a love/hate, father/daughter kind of thing.

At that point, one of the firefighters simply picked Barbara up and carried her away from the wreckage, bringing her over to where Mel and I had taken refuge on a piece of sidewalk slick with shattered glass. "Keep her here and get her shoes back on," the man growled at us. "We need this woman out of our way!"

Another firefighter appeared behind him. "Okay," he said. "We've got permission to land the chopper on top of KOMO."

The snarl of traffic, growing worse by the minute, made transporting Harry to a hospital by ambulance a nonstarter. The building for the local ABC affiliate, complete with a helipad on its roof, was almost directly across the street. In moments, they had Harry out of the crushed vehicle and onto a gurney, rolling him across the street and toward the building to the helipad. Once at Harborview Hospital, a team of the ER docs tried valiantly to save his legs. It didn't work. His legs were gone, and soon, so was everything else, S.H.I.T included.

Within weeks of Ross Connors's funeral and while Harry was still in the hospital, the governor—the one from the "other side of the aisle"—had appointed a new attorney general, whose first order of business was to disband Special Homicide altogether. Suddenly we were all out of a job. Well, not all of us. Mel was one of the younger ones, and she'd already decided to make the move to Bellingham before the axe fell. But the rest of us—the old duffers—were out of luck. For right now, I was keeping busy wrangling construction projects. What I'd do later on when all the plaster dust settled was something I mostly avoided contemplating.

I found a parking place on Cherry and trudged half a block in the wrong direction to find the applicable pay station, grumbling to myself the whole way about the loss of old-fashioned parking meters. They might have eaten every bit of change out of your pocket in the blink of an eye, but at least they were right there by your car. You didn't have to go searching for them.

I was back on Boren and about to walk through the automatic doors into the lobby, when Harry hailed me by name. Turning, I saw his wheelchair parked some fifty feet away from the door under a bus-stop-like shelter designed to keep smokers away from the building and out of the rain, at least, if not out of the cold. I had wheeled him up there more than once, so he could have a smoke.

Coming closer, I saw that Harry wasn't alone. Standing nearby was Marge Herndon herself, the hoyden who had looked after me during my bout with postsurgical rehab. She was smoking like a chimney, and so was Harry. He looked happier than I'd seen him in months.

"Hey," he said, waving his burning cigarette in her direction. "Thanks for putting me in touch with Margie here. She came by just now to introduce herself. She got here a few minutes early. The woman is a gem."

Are you kidding? They'd barely been introduced, and Harry was already calling her Margie? I had known the woman for months without ever getting beyond the basic

Nurse Ratched stage. And he thought she was a "gem"? I regarded the woman as an absolute terror, one who had run roughshod over me for what had seemed like months rather than weeks.

I nodded in Marge's direction. "Good to see you," I said.

"Same here," she muttered tersely in a way that told me that even though Harry had scored big with her, I had not.

I knew in that moment that, once again, Mel had been right, and I was wrong. In the course of a single cigarette, or maybe two, Marge Herndon had Harry I. Ball eating out of her hand.

It was enough to piss off the Good Fairy.

Clearly, since Marge and Harry were getting along like gangbusters, my planned introduction as well as my continued presence weren't required. I chatted for a few minutes, then, excusing myself, I found my car, complete with paid-for-but-unused parking time, and made my way down the hill to I-5, where I headed north.

JIM HUNT HAD located three possible contractors for us. This one, Don Hastings, the last one on the list, lived in Smoky Point, a tiny ex-burb north of Everett.

Don had done jobs for Jim Hunt several times in the past, and he and his people had done quality work. He had also handled projects in towns stretching from Everett all the way to the Canadian border. That meant he had contacts and working relationships with people in planning departments from here to there. Those connections were bound to streamline the permitting process. More to the point, he had a crew based in Arlington that was finishing up one job and would be ready to tackle another within a matter of weeks.

We'd taken proposals from the two other construction outfits—so we had three estimates altogether. Jim had warned us that the one from Hastings would most likely come in as the priciest one of the three in terms of up-front cost, but I've learned over time that you get what you pay for. And I'd already made up my mind to sign on the dotted line long before I found my way to Don's office, located in a converted garage next to his residence on the outskirts of town. I stayed long enough to meet the man in person and write a deposit check that would put the wheels in motion, then I headed north again, leaving Don and Jim Hunt huddled together over a stack of plans spread out across a drafting table.

Once on I-5, I tried calling Mel to let her know the deed was done, but when her phone went straight to voice mail, I didn't bother leaving a message. She was probably busy, and I'd be there soon enough to give her the news in person.

Although I was glad to have the project out of my hands and in the care and keeping of a competent professional, I was a little blue about it, too. I had been so preoccupied with dealing with the housing issues that I'd had little time to think about what I was going to do with the rest of my life.

Between my years at Seattle P.D. and the ones with S.H.I.T., I'd spent almost all my adult life in law enforcement. It's not just a career. It's a mind-set and a way of life. There are far too many stories out there of ex-cops who, having pulled the plug on working, end up taking their own lives. Of course, that wouldn't be me. For starters, I had Mel. I was determined to spend every possible moment with her. She had her own career path now—a complicated career path—but what the hell was I supposed to do with my spare time? Take up golf, for Pete's sake? That seemed to be working for my friend, Ralph Ames who, along with his wife, Mary, was now living— and golfing—at a development called Pebble Creek which is somewhere in the Phoenix metropolitan area. Ralph had tried unsuccessfully to interest me in golfing. It just didn't take.

Twenty miles out of Bellingham, I dialed Mel's number again. This time I did leave a message. "Hey," I said. "I signed the contract with Don Hastings. Things moved faster than I expected. Since I'm sort of in the neighborhood, I thought I'd see if we could grab a quick late lunch. Call me when you have time. I'm about twenty minutes out."

It was frustrating to know that Mel was in a complicated situation at work and that, other than offering her moral support, there was little I could do about it. As far as I could tell, Mel's tenure as chief had been completely devoid of a honeymoon period. It had become clear all too soon that Mel's selection by the city council and city manager had been made over the mayor's strenuous objections. Mayor Adelina Kirkpatrick was a typical small-time politician. The mayor was a lifelong Bellingham resident who knew where all the bodies were buried while

Mel was new to town. Mel had learned that the mayor had fully expected Assistant Chief Austin Manson to be handed the job of chief, a move that had been thwarted by both the city manager and the city council. That meant Mel's relationship with the mayor had started out on the wrong foot and had stayed that way.

Midway through Mel's second week in office, there had been an officer-involved shooting in Bellingham at a lowlife bar on the waterfront, a rough place called the Fish Bowl. For most of my working life, that term—the Fish Bowl— had referred to the window-lined office on the fifth floor of Seattle's Public Safety Building where Homicide Captain Larry Powell long held sway. So the irony of the bar's name touched my funny bone. On the surface, the shoot-out shouldn't have been all that serious. For one thing, nobody died.

Mel had been locked up in a meeting with the mayor and the city manager at the time of the incident. At the mayor's insistence, pagers and other electronic devices were not allowed inside her office. That struck me as odd all by itself. I warned Mel that anyone that concerned about electronic eavesdropping was either a conspiracy freak or else s/he had something to hide. As far as Mayor Kirkpatrick was concerned, it might have been a little of both.

Some people stream music on their phones and tablets. Once Mel ended up in Bellingham, I spent a lot of time tuned into a radio station there. I also programmed my iPad so breaking news alerts from there would be sent to me as they occurred. The day of the shooting, with Mel locked in the mayor's office, I knew about the incident before she did. As soon as the news alert showed up on my screen, my heart went to my throat. As police chief, Mel shouldn't have been out on any kind of patrol, still I didn't breathe easier until I had called her office, checked with her secretary, and learned that Mel was still upstairs in a meeting. Whew!

Over the course of time—that day and subsequent ones—the details emerged. A young cop, Officer Dale Embry, had been patrolling the waterfront area when a guy came running out of the Fish Bowl and flagged him down, alerting him to a developing domestic-violence situation inside the bar. Embry radioed for backup then hurried inside. The bartender's estranged and enraged husband, armed with a butcher knife, was threatening to murder his soon-to-be-former wife and anyone stupid enough to get in his way.

Embry entered the premises with his weapon already drawn. When Embry told the guy to drop his knife, the guy swung around and started for him. I know firsthand that when you're facing an assailant armed with a knife, you're caught in a chaotic situation, and you're not exactly thinking straight. Adrenaline is pumping; your heart is hammering off the charts, and you're hoping to God it's not your last day on planet earth.

Embry pulled the trigger. The shot should have taken the guy down. It didn't, but only because someone else took him down first. One of the customers, armed with a barstool, clobbered the irate husband and put him on the floor. The only other casualty turned out to be the mirror behind the bar, which shattered into a million pieces.

The assailant was knocked out cold. An ambulance was summoned and hauled him off to the ER with a possible concussion. When departmental supervisors arrived on the scene, a group that ultimately included Assistant Chief Manson, Officer Embry was sent home on administrative leave.

In officer-involved shootings where a weapon is discharged, administrative leave is standard procedure. When Mel came out of her meeting, however, and learned it was a done deal, she was not pleased. Yes, she hadn't had her pager along in the meeting, but she was offended that Manson hadn't bothered to come upstairs himself or even send someone up to let her know about the incident while it was still unfolding. She took the position that, by issuing the leave order himself, Manson had undercut her authority.

In the heat of the moment, she had called Assistant Chief Manson out about it and given him a dressing-down. Later on that day, she paid a call at Officer Embry's home, encouraging him to use his leave time constructively in a way that would turn him into a better cop. After that visit, she had attempted to apologize to Manson, but he wasn't having any of it. The damage was done. Manson was pissed, and apparently he planned to stay that way.

The problem was, I could see both sides of the issue. This was a routine situation and a routine call on Manson's part. If Mel had been a more seasoned chief, she wouldn't have felt compelled to assert her authority in such a heavy-handed fashion. Perhaps she shouldn't have reacted the way she did initially, but now it was too late. Rather than having Manson as an ally, she had turned the man into a sworn enemy.

When Mel had accepted the job, I think she had imagined herself as being the kind of skilled leader Ross Connors had always been. The problem was, when it came to building S.H.I.T., Ross Connors had been able to go out and handpick the people he wanted on his team. It had been an older, wiser, and dedicated group, with little, if any, deadweight. In her new department, Mel didn't have the luxury of handpicking her people. She had to work with what was already there.

Two months later, Embry was back from his leave. Due to the Fish Bowl incident, Mel was stuck with both an extremely loyal but peach-fuzzed young cop and a grizzled veteran who wouldn't give her the time of day and didn't miss a trick when it came to badmouthing Mel behind her back. In terms of departmental morale, guess which one carries more weight?

One evening, over dinner, I had made the tactical error of venturing an opinion on the subject. As a result, Assistant Chief Manson was no longer a topic of conversation between Mel and me. He was the elephant in the room—the taboo place where neither of us dared to tread.

I was coming up on the Fairhaven exit when I tried Mel's phone one last time. By then, I was slightly annoyed. Obviously, my idea of treating her to a surprise lunch wasn't going to happen. Consequently, I turned on the directional signal. Exiting the freeway, I left another message.

"You're probably too busy for lunch," I said. "There's no sense in my coming down to the department and being under hand and foot. I'm turning off at Fairhaven. I'll wait at the house until you get cut loose. Maybe I can take you out to dinner instead of lunch. If you're really lucky, you might even talk me into spending the night."

I drove over to Bayside and down the steep driveway that leads to our house. Mel's Porsche Cayman was tucked in behind a massive construction Dumpster that had taken over a big portion of the concrete slab that had once been a detached garage. The rest of the garage structure, afflicted by a terminal case of dry rot, had been redflagged as a hazard, knocked down, and the splintered remains hauled away during the first week of our renovation efforts. Mel had worried that perhaps it was an omen about the inadvisability of the entire project. Jim Hunt had attempted to reassure her by explaining that in sixty-year-old wood-frame buildings, dry rot was simply the natural order of things, especially in the rainy Pacific Northwest.

I wasn't surprised to find her car parked there. Mel had told me that when things got too stressful at work, she'd grab a sandwich from Subway and drive out to our place, where she would eat lunch in her car, take a few deep breaths, and relieve the pressure by watching the birds out on the bay. I suspected that once the workers showed up, and construction kicked into high gear, parking there for lunch wouldn't be nearly as peaceful.

Given all that, I half expected to see her sitting in the car, but she wasn't, so I walked on down to the front of the house and stepped up onto the sagging front porch. The door was locked, so I used the key and stepped inside.

"Mel?" I called into the echoing skeletal shell. "Are you here?"

She wasn't. The house was empty. Leaving the front door ajar, I went back outside and walked across the sloping front yard until I came to a halt at the fence that marked the end of our property.

"Mel?" I called down the bluff, "where are you?" Again, there was no answer.

Mel is physically fit, but clambering around on a steep hillside even in a uniform and low heels didn't seem in character unless, of course, someone else had been in trouble. Then all bets were off. For the first time, I felt the smallest frisson of concern.

"Mel," I called again, shouting this time. I peered off down the bank. At the condo in Seattle, we keep two pairs of binoculars parked on the sill next to the window seat. We used them for occasional bits of bird-watching, for viewing the Fourth of July Fireworks, and occasionally, during snowstorms, for being entertained while watching hapless drivers attempt to make their fender-bender way up and down Broad. Unfortunately, I didn't have a pair of binoculars here with me now at a time and place where I really needed them.

If a boat had overturned, I knew Mel would have wanted to lend a hand, but it seemed unlikely that she would have gone down the bank on foot. It seemed far more reasonable that she would have used her phone to summon help. Besides, there was no sign of wreckage out on the water or on the steep bank at the water's edge. And no sign of life either—no sign of movement.

There was a rough, steep trail that ran in breathtaking switchbacks down to the water. It might have been usable by mountain goats, but I didn't think it was something that should be tackled by an old codger with a pair of fake knees. When I walked over to the path and studied it closely, I saw no sign of any recent footprints. If Mel had gone down the bluff, she hadn't used the path.

I stood up and looked down at the bay again. There was a stiff wind blowing in off the water. The sky above may have been a robin's egg blue, but the sea itself was gray-green and dotted with rolling whitecaps. It looked dangerous—and threatening.

Genuinely worried now and still staring down the hillside for any sign of movement, I plucked my phone out of my pocket and dialed Mel's cell phone again—with predictable results. The call went straight to voice mail. Then I dialed Mel's office, not her direct line, but the one that was usually answered by Kelly, the receptionist stationed just outside Mel's door.

"Is Chief Soames in?" I asked when Kelly answered. "This is her husband calling."

"No, she isn't here," Kelly answered, "and I'm a little surprised. She was supposed to do a live radio interview at one. I've tried calling her cell, but she doesn't answer. It's not like her to miss an appointment like this."

No it's not, I thought grimly. "If you do hear from her," I said aloud, "ask her to give me a call."

Before ringing off, I gave Kelly my cell-phone number,

then I hurried back up the hill. Ignoring the wide-open front door, I headed straight for the back of the house and to the spot where the cars were parked, with mine directly behind hers. Some ancient cop instinct must have kicked in. As I approached her vehicle, rather than grabbing the door handle and pulling it open, I bent down and shaded my face enough so I could peer inside.

That's when my heart almost came to a stop. Mel's purse lay half-open on the passenger seat. Next to it lay an unopened Subway sandwich—her favorite, no doubt, tuna with jack cheese and jalapeños. Next to the sandwich, I caught sight of what looked like the grip of a weapon. Her Smith & Wesson maybe? There was her cell phone, too, but what really took my breath away was what I saw on the passenger floorboard—a shoe—a single, abandoned shoe, one of the low-heeled black pumps Mel routinely wore to work. If she had been in the driver's seat, and the shoe was in the passenger footwell, that indicated there must have been a struggle of some kind.

I stepped away from the vehicle without touching it—holding my hands in the air as though I'd been ordered to do so by a traffic cop. If something had happened to Mel—if someone had forced her out of her vehicle—I had to stop being a worried husband and transform myself into a detective. I looked around. The cars were parked below the crest of the hill out of view from the level above and shielded from the neighbors on either side by a thick screen of trees. It seemed unlikely that there would have been anyone close enough to witness whatever had happened.

Fighting panic, I fumbled to pry my cell phone from my pocket. My fingers seemed like frozen stubs as I forced them to dial.

"Nine-one-one," a calm-voiced woman answered. "What is your emergency?"

"It's my wife," I said. "I think someone's taken her."

"What do you mean by 'taken?'" she asked.

I tried to keep my voice steady. "My wife is Mel Soames," I said. "She's the police chief here in Bellingham, and she's missing."

"Calm down, sir. What do you mean 'missing'?"

I wanted to reach through the phone and throttle the woman. How could she be so stupid?

"I mean her car is here. Her purse is here. Her weapon is here. She isn't. I think she's been kidnapped."

"Where are you?" the operator asked.

Taking a deep breath to control my temper, I gave her the address. "All right," the woman said. "I'm sending units your way. Do you have any idea how long she's been gone?"

I walked around to the front of the Porsche and leaned over close enough to the hood to hear if there was any clicking from the engine. There was nothing—not a sound—and there wasn't any heat rising from the hood, either. That meant that the car had been parked long enough for the engine to cool completely.

"No idea," I said into the phone, "but probably an hour at least."

While waiting for a patrol car to arrive and to avoid disturbing any possible evidence, I forced myself to stay away from the vehicle. I walked past the house, through the front yard, and all the way back down to the fence, where I stood stock-still, staring out to sea. Anyone seeing me right then might have assumed I was simply admiring the water view. I wasn't. I was peering into an abyss at the appalling possibility of losing what I held most dear and knowing that if Mel was lost, I was, too.

That's when it hit me. If a woman goes missing, who's the first suspect? The husband or else the person who calls it in. In this instance, that would be yours truly twice over. I thought about how I had forced myself to sound calm during the 9-1-1 call, and then I thought about all the other 9-1-1 recordings I had heard over the years—the ones where some chump calls to report that he found his dead wife, the wife he just murdered, lying on the floor in the living room. Usually, the killer will mention that he's tried reviving her even though the autopsy will reveal that she died hours before the 9-1-1 call. Instead of trying to bring her around, he's spent the interim attempting to clean up the crime scene.

I was that guy now, the calm one on the phone. When officers did show up, I'd be the first one they interviewed and the first one under suspicion. I knew what that meant, too. While investigators were busy investigating me, whoever had done it would have plenty of time to get away.

That thought brought me up short. Who had done it? Was the unknown assailant someone who just happened to come by? Was this a crime of opportunity, or was it something else, something planned and deliberate? And if it was the latter, who had it in for Mel Soames.

I could think of only one answer to that question—the guy who had been passed over for the job of chief, Austin Manson. Mel's phone was there in the car. Otherwise, I could have used our Find My Device app to locate her. But what about Manson, where was he, and, if he was the culprit, was Mel still with him?

The house was at the far southern end of Bellingham in a low-crime area. That explained why it was taking time for a patrol car to arrive on the scene. I took out my phone again and redialed Mel's office. "I'm looking for Austin Manson," I told Kelly, identifying myself again and hoping against hope that word of my 9-1-1 call hadn't yet filtered upstairs from the emergency operator.

"Sorry, Assistant Chief Manson is out sick today," Kelly informed me. "Can anyone else help you?"

I'm not generally a very good liar, but right then that's exactly what I needed to be—a capable and believable liar. "I wanted to surprise Mel by inviting Assistant Chief Manson to dinner with us tomorrow night," I said. "Do you happen to have either a home number for him or else a cell?"

Kelly gave me both, texting them to me because I had no other way to write them down. Did I turn around and try calling either one? No, I did not. Instead, my next call was placed to a guy named Todd Hatcher.

Todd is a self-styled forensic economist whose playbook includes access to untold databases. He also has an uncanny way with computers. In S.H.I.T., Todd had functioned as Ross Connors's unseen right-hand man, and now Todd was the one I turned to for help.

"Hey," Todd said when he answered the phone. I could hear the noisy sound of a child wailing somewhere near the background—most likely Todd and Julie's two-year-old daughter, Danielle. "Long time no see."

A momentary silence followed. I was remembering the last several times I'd seen Todd—first in the flashing-light chaos beneath the Space Needle minutes after Ross Connors's car wreck; at the funeral for Bill Spade, Ross's driver; and finally outside the packed gymnasium at O'Dea High School, which had been the only place deemed large enough to hold Ross Connors's funeral. From the odd catch in Todd's voice when he spoke again, I suspect he was recalling those same scenes.

"What's up?"

Standing in the chilly midday sunlight, I heard the distant sound of an approaching siren. There wasn't much time. I told him what I needed as quickly as I could.

"You think this sour-grapes guy Manson may be behind what's happened?"

"I do. He called in sick today. If I try to tell one of his officers that I think the assistant chief is the one responsible for all this, the cop will most likely fall on the floor laughing. Maybe I'm wrong. Maybe Manson isn't behind it at all, but I still want to know where he is as of right now."

"Beau," Todd began, "do you think . . . ?" I could hear the coming barrage of caution before Todd ever managed to spit it out, and I cut him off in midsentence.

"I'm texting you his numbers right now," I told him urgently. "Please, Todd, see if you can locate Manson's cell."

"As long as we don't have a warrant, anything you find won't hold up in court."

"Mel's life is in danger. That means we can get around the need for a warrant. Besides, I'm not a cop any longer," I snarled at him. "I don't give a rat's ass about admissible evidence."

I disconnected then, forwarded the numbers to him, and started back up the slope, just as a patrol car came down the driveway and screeched to a stop with one final bleat from the siren.

When the cop emerged from the car, I took a look at his baby face and figured he would be something less than useless. Then I saw his name tag—Officer Dale Embry—the young guy from that officer-involved shooting months earlier. I don't know how many sworn officers there are in Mel's department, but when I realized who he was, I felt as though I had just won the lottery.

"What seems to be the problem?" Embry asked.

"It's my wife," I said, pointing at Mel's car. "I think she's been kidnapped."

There probably aren't that many Caymans running loose in Bellingham. As soon as Embry glanced at the vehicle, a look of shocked recognition spread across his features. He immediately spoke into the radio attached to the shoulder of his uniform.

"Officer needs assistance," he said. "Chief Soames is missing."

I'm not sure if the emergency operator had deliberately withheld that piece of information from her radio transmission or if it had simply been an oversight on her part, but I knew Embry's call would bring a stampede of officers, most likely none of whom would turn out to be Assistant Chief Manson. I also knew that if I let my car be trapped in the driveway, it might take hours for me to get it loose again. I couldn't risk that.

"Let me move my vehicle out of the way so the detectives and CSIs can access her car."

Embry was very young, bless his heart—young and naive. I learned later that he was also an Eagle Scout and a Boy Scout troop leader. He hadn't yet learned that most people can look you straight in the eye and lie through their teeth. The prospect that his chief had been kidnapped left him totally out of his depth, so he was happy to let me. Once back up on street level, I heard the sounds of multiple sirens approaching, and so I simply vanished, driving out of the Bayside neighborhood and slipping quietly into the parking lot of a nearby apartment building. I was gone before any other officers arrived on the scene. With any kind of luck, it would be quite some time before Embry figured out that I hadn't come back down the driveway along with everybody else.

I'm not a man given to praying, but that's what I did—I prayed my heart out. I was still in the apartment parking lot and in the middle of my long heart-to-heart chat with the Man Upstairs when my phone rang, with Todd Hatcher on the line.

"That was quick," I said.

"Completely illegal but quick," he responded. "I got a ping off Manson's phone. He's currently in the parking lot of the scenic overlook at a place called Larrabee State Park. It's on Highway 11, about six miles south of Fairhaven at milepost fourteen. Depending on how fast you drive, it should take ten to fifteen minutes to get there."

"I'm on my way. What kind of vehicle does Manson drive?"

"I thought you'd want to know that," Todd said, "and I have it for you. It's an '06 Chevrolet Malibu."

During that drive, Formula 1 drivers had nothing on me. I made it to the overlook parking lot in just under seven minutes. Driving there, I realized it was probably close to the same spot where Mel, while working for S.H.I.T, had located the remains of a missing guy who'd fallen to his death on a Sunday afternoon while taking a leak on his way home from an afternoon of heavy drinking.

Somewhere along the way, I realized that I'd gone off and left the front door to the house unlocked and wide open. With cops all over the place, I didn't suppose that was much of a problem, for the remainder of the afternoon anyway. Besides, since the place had already been stripped bare in preparation for the remodel, how much damage could anyone do?

Todd had said that the overlook was right around milepost fourteen. I slowed down about a half a mile out so I could approach the place under the flag of your ordinary day-tripper out seeing the sights. When I pulled into the parking lot, there were only two other vehicles visible. One was a white Chevy Malibu, parked at the far end of the lot. In the middle of the space was an immense luxury tour-bus loaded with a group of Japanese tourists, who were in the process of cleaning up after a chilly, windblown picnic lunch. Pretending to throw away some trash, I blended in with the group and discovered that most of them spoke English surprisingly well. I engaged a couple of them in conversation long enough to learn that they had spent the weekend sightseeing at the Skagit Valley Tulip Festival. Now they were taking the scenic route north to Vancouver, B.C., before catching their flight back to Tokyo.

I usually grumble about tourists. The hordes of camera-wielding dolts who stream off cruise ships and into downtown Seattle and the Regrade these days can be downright provoking. They may drop millions of dollars into the cash registers of local merchants, but my big gripe is that they tend to walk four and five abreast, effectively blocking traffic on any given sidewalk at any given time.

This particular batch of tourists, however, I regarded as an absolute godsend. Manson had probably come here thinking he'd have plenty of time and privacy to send Mel plunging from the parking lot to certain death on the wave-pounded rocks far below. My hope—my slenderest smidgen of hope—was that the picnickers had delayed him long enough that Mel was still alive.

A man I suspected of being the tour-bus driver stood off by himself, smoking a cigarette. The passengers might have been Japanese, but I could tell by his flannel shirt and baseball cap that the driver was dyed-in-the-wool American.

Taking a steadying breath, I walked toward him, not knowing as I went what I would say or even exactly what I wanted to accomplish. On the one hand, having the tourists present provided cover for me and kept Manson from making his next move. On the other hand, I was armed, and, most likely, Manson was, too. If the confrontation ended up turning into some kind of shoot-out, I didn't want to be responsible for putting a busload of innocent Japanese visitors in jeopardy.

The driver stubbed out his cigarette as I approached. "How's it going?" he said.

Those three words were ordinary enough—casually welcoming of a stranger, but, at the same time, a bit on the wary side, as though to say he thought I might turn out to be an okay guy while still warning me not to try getting too chummy. I needed a quick way to start a conversation, and so, even though I quit smoking literally decades ago, I came up with the only possible topic that had any hope of working.

"Got a smoke?" I asked.

There's an instant bonding among smokers these days. Smokers are so accustomed to being treated like pariahs—glared at, ridiculed, and reviled—that when they find other like-minded individuals, they tend to let down their defenses. I had seen that phenomenon at work earlier that very morning in the interaction between Harry I. Ball and Marge Herndon. They met, they lit their respective cigarettes, and were instantly pals for life.

After a moment's hesitation, the driver reached into his pocket and pulled out a pack of cigarettes—a brand I didn't recognize. From an arm's length away, I could see that the writing on the package was in Japanese. What I couldn't see from that distance was if the indecipherable characters included any of our country's nanny-state grim health warnings.

"A gift from one of my passengers," he explained, noticing that I was studying the packaging. "They brought their own along on the trip, and that's a good thing. It means they don't mind if I stop for cigarette breaks. They want them, too."

He tapped a cigarette out and held the package in my direction. Then he took one for himself and lit both with a lighter he extracted from the pocket of his jeans.

I took a puff. After so many years of not smoking, that first fiery lungful of nicotine hit me like a ton of bricks. It took real effort on my part to suppress a sudden fit of coughing.

"I've got a problem," I said.

"Oh, yeah?" Cigarette bonding goes only so far. Wariness crept back into his voice. "Like what?"

"You see that car over there in the corner?"

"You mean the Malibu with the guy sitting in it? He showed up a while ago. He's been sitting there the whole time without getting out of the car. Made me wonder what he was up to."

"And well you should," I told him. "The guy behind the wheel works with my wife and hates her guts. She's gone missing. I think he might have kidnapped her from our new house in Fairhaven. I believe she's locked in the trunk and that he brought her here to kill her. As soon as he has a chance, I suspect he's going to shove her off the cliff."

That declaration provoked a fit of coughing—from the driver, this time, rather than from me. "You're kidding," he gasped when the spasm subsided. "It's March. What is this, some kind of weird April Fool's joke?"

"It's no joke. My name is J. P. Beaumont. I'm a retired homicide cop. My wife's name is Melissa Soames, but she goes by Mel. She was recently appointed chief of police in Bellingham. Austin Manson is her second-in-command. He's pissed beyond measure that she got the top job, and he didn't. He's known to have a temper."

"Pissed enough to kill her?" the driver said, shaking his head in disbelief. "No way!"

"Way," I said.

"If he kidnapped her, how come you know about it? What makes you think he brought her here?"

"We got a ping off his cell phone."

The driver ground out the remains of his half-smoked cigarette. "I'd better get my people out of here pronto," he said. "Before the cops show up, and this our picnic turns into the shoot-out at the OK Corral."

"Wait," I said. "Please. I need your help."

He gave me what Jeremy, my son-in-law, calls the stink-eye. "What kind of help?"

"The fact that you and your people have been here is probably the only thing keeping him from making a move. I need you to stay. Round up your people. Get them loaded onto the bus, but please don't leave. If things go to hell in a handbasket, and there is a shoot-out, chances are we're talking handguns. I doubt he'll be armed with a high-powered rifle. Your bus should be far enough away that the passengers shouldn't be in any danger."

"But they might be," the driver pointed out.

"Yes," I agreed. "They could be."

"You and he might be armed with handguns only," the driver continued, "but the cops who show up will come with rifles and shotguns at the ready and with bulletproof vests, besides. My poor people have nothing," he added, nodding in the general direction of the bus. "Zilch. They'll be sitting ducks."

This was the part where things were getting dicey—the place where I would either lose him completely or win him over. It could go either way.

"The cops aren't coming," I said. "As I said, I'm Mel's husband. Right now, I'm most likely suspect *numero uno* as far as the cops are concerned. They're probably searching for me high and low."

"They don't know you're here?"

I shook my head. "The problem is, while everybody else is wasting their time looking for me, I'm afraid Manson is going to kill her. You and I may be her only chance."

I said my piece then fell silent and waited. For a long time, the only sound in the graveled parking lot was the soft roar of waves breaking on rocks far below. I was afraid he would simply turn and walk away. He didn't. Straightening his shoulders, he looked me square in the eye.

"What do you need me to do?"

It was all I could do to keep from hugging the guy. I said, "Get your passengers loaded into the bus. Tell them to take cover as best they can—to sink down below window level as much as possible."

The driver grinned then. "That shouldn't be a problem. Most of 'em aren't any bigger than a minute."

"By the way, could you lend me another cigarette?"

"Lend?" he replied. "Are you saying you'll buy me a pack when all this is over?"

The cigarette-smoker's bonding was back, big-time. The driver and I were on the same page. We were a team. He pulled out his pack and passed me a single cigarette.

"Pack? Hell," I declared, "I'll buy you a whole damned carton."

"What are you going to do?"

"I'm going to walk over there, tap on the window, and ask for a light."

"If he works with your wife, won't he recognize you?"

"I doubt it. Manson knows Mel; he doesn't know me. We've never met. When he rolls down the window, I'm going to take him down. While I'm doing that, you get on the horn to 9-1-1. Tell them there's some kind of altercation going down here at the state park. You're welcome to say I'm involved or not, your call. Say you believe people's lives are in danger and to get here fast."

There was a pause. Finally, he said, "What if things don't go your way?"

"Then take your bus and your people and get the hell out of here because if I don't succeed in nailing the bastard, my wife's done for, and so am I."

After an even longer pause, the driver nodded and held out his hand. We shook. "Good luck," he said. "I'm rooting for you."

With that, he headed for his bus, and I turned toward the Malibu. It was parked at the far south end of the lot, with the passenger side snug up against a guardrail made of a long length of log rather than metal. Given the distance down the cliff on the far side of that slender barrier, I would have much preferred metal.

Forcing myself not to rush, I sauntered up to the Malibu's driver-side door and rapped sharply on the glass with one hand while holding up a cigarette in the other. Then I bent down and mouthed three understated words through the closed window, "Got a light?"

Before Manson could reply, I slipped my right hand into my jacket pocket and closed my fingers around the plastic grip on my Glock. Manson must have been dozing when I tapped on the window. He started awake at the sudden noise and reached for something I couldn't see—a gun most likely. After a moment and to my immense relief, he seemed to relax. The window rolled down.

Manson looked at me through bloodshot eyes. "Whaddyu want?" he demanded as a blast of boozy breath spilled out of the car, leaving its stink in the cool, crisp air around us.

I reasoned that if Manson was going to shoot first and ask questions later, he would have done so already. Luckily for me, the bus was still there and still acting as a deterrent because it meant there were all kinds of possible witnesses on the scene. Even drunk as a skunk, Manson knew better than to gun someone down in cold blood in front of a spellbound audience.

"Got a light?" I repeated. "I must have blown a fuse or two in my Mercedes. Neither of my lighters work, and I'm dying for a smoke."

Manson gave an exaggerated sigh, then he reached over and punched the lighter button on his dashboard. With his right hand. Amen! That probably meant he was right-handed. It also meant that a hand holding a lit lighter wouldn't be holding a gun. Couldn't be holding a gun. I studied him while we waited for the lighter to heat up. Manson was in his midfifties, wore his hair in a graying crew cut, and was reasonably fit. He could have been me a few years ago, up to and including the booze-fueled breath.

I waited until he held out the lighter, then I pounced. I dropped the cigarette, grabbed his wrist with both hands, and twisted for all I was worth. Then I bodily dragged his resisting body out through the open window.

"What the hell?" he yelled, fighting to free himself. "Let go. I'll kill you, you asshole."

Manson's big problem right then was that he was still drunk, and I wasn't. I dropped him onto the ground from window height and heard the air swoosh out of his lungs. Once he was on the ground gasping for breath, I was there, too, twisting his arm into an impossible pretzel behind his back in a way that was only a half inch short of pulling his shoulder out of its socket.

"You bastard," he howled when he could speak again "Whoever you are, you are a dead man."

"No, I'm not, Manson," I told him cheerfully, "but you're done. Stand down!"

Out of the corner of my eye, I saw the bus driver sprinting toward us from across the parking lot. "Thought you could use these," he said, arriving out of breath and gasping but holding up a handful of industrial sized tie-wraps. "You'd be surprised how often they come in handy on the bus. And I called the cops just like you said. They're on their way."

Moments later, with both of Manson's hands properly cuffed behind his back, I stood up, more grateful than ever for Dr. Auld, the orthopedic surgeon over at Swedish Hospital who had replaced my original out-of-warranty knees with properly working new ones. Manson was still on the ground, grumbling and railing. Meanwhile, I slipped the Glock out of my jacket pocket and back into its holster. No shots had been fired. There was no reason to have a weapon on display when the cavalry showed up.

That's about the time I first heard a fierce thumping noise coming from inside the trunk. Mel was alive! Tears of relief sprang from my eyes as I searched the interior of the Malibu for the trunk release. A second later, the bus driver and I stood in front of the open trunk, staring down at my wife. She was alive but helpless, duct-taped from head to foot. A long strip of tape covered her mouth. It hurt me to pull the sticky gag as well as a layer of skin off her face, but it didn't bother her. In fact, I don't think she even noticed.

"Where's Manson?" she demanded furiously, once she

was free of the gag. "Just wait until I get my hands on that bastard!"

"Manson is handled," I assured her. "He's not in custody just yet, but he's handled. What about you? Are you all right? Are you hurt?"

Still focused on Manson, she didn't answer, but as I helped her sit up, I saw a streak of dried blood that ran from her right temple all the way to her chin. Most likely, Manson had used something heavy to clock her over the head and knock her out.

While I loosened the restraints on Mel's legs, peeling off strips of shredded panty hose along with every piece of duct tape, the bus driver worked at freeing her hands. Once Mel was free from the tape, we attempted to stand her upright, but she immediately toppled over. Luckily, we caught her before she landed on her face. Her lower limbs were so numb, it was impossible for her to stand on her own.

"Who's this?" she asked, nodding toward the driver, who was gripping her other elbow.

"Name's Sam," he told her with a grin. "That's my bus over there. I'm the bus driver."

"Today I think Sam is short for Good Samaritan," Mel declared.

We all laughed uproariously at that, as though she had just cracked the best joke ever, and maybe she had. Then, as suddenly as our outburst of laughter had erupted, it ended. Limp with relief, Mel fell weeping against my shoulder. "Manson was going to kill me," she sobbed brokenly. "He said if he couldn't have the job, I sure as hell wouldn't have it, either."

"I know," I murmured comfortingly into her ear. "I know."

I tried to pretend I was holding her tightly against me in order to keep her from falling, but that wasn't the only reason—not by a long shot. I didn't want to let go of her ever again.

After a time, she pried herself loose from my grasp. "Where are we?" she asked, frowning.

"Larrabee Park on Chuckanut Drive, a few miles south of Fairhaven."

"How did you find me?" she wanted to know. "How did you know to come here?"

I didn't answer the question, but she figured it out anyway. "Todd?" she asked a moment later.

I nodded.

"And he located Manson's cell phone without having a warrant?"

I nodded again.

"Well," she said, "we can't just throw him under the bus, can we?"

When Sam objected to her use of that particular terminology, Mel quickly corrected herself. "I mean, we can't tell the cops about any of this. If they find out what Todd can do, they'll be all over him. He might even end up in jail."

"You're right," I agreed. "It's probably for best if we don't make any mention of him or his participation."

"What then?" Mel asked. She fell silent, but soon she brightened. "Wait a minute," she said. "I know how to handle this."

Reaching into the jacket pocket of her very rumpled uniform, she pulled out a spare set of keys. Mel Soames is notorious for losing track of keys—car keys, house keys, you name it. As a consequence, she never goes anywhere without two complete sets—one in her purse and one in her pocket. She held the key ring up, in the air jingling it triumphantly in front of my face. "We'll tell them you used this."

Months earlier, for Christmas, I had given her a collection of small squares of plastic tiles, containing locator chips. With the devices attached to her key rings, no matter where she misplaced one of them, we could use our iPhones to find it.

"Those are designed to work inside houses or apartments," I objected. "It would never cover this much distance."

"Technology is mysterious," Mel declared. "Nobody else knows that for sure, and what they don't know won't hurt them."

Sam saw that as a signal to take his leave. "I'd better go check on my passengers and let them know everything's all right," he said, backing away from us.

It was a good thing we'd already made arrangements about handling the locator beacon because, at that point, a string of cop cars with lights flashing and sirens blaring came streaming into the parking lot. Someone grabbed up

Austin Manson and hustled him away, first into the back of a patrol car and later into a newly arrived ambulance.

I expected that investigators would immediately separate Mel and me while someone else went to talk to Sam. That's what cops usually do—they separate witnesses and suspects in an effort to keep them from comparing notes and collaborating as far as their various stories are concerned. I was grateful that Mel and I had managed to get our stories straight before the new arrivals got there.

But before we could be separated and interviewed, something unexpected happened. A white Buick sedan nosed its way into the crush of cop cars, and a woman I later learned was Mayor Kirkpatrick bounded out of the car and started throwing around her considerable weight. I have no idea how she learned about what was going on as fast as she did. Maybe she was monitoring police scanners. Maybe someone called her directly to let her know.

She hustled up to Detective Walsh, the officer in charge. "Is it true?" she demanded. "Is Austin Manson behind all this?"

Walsh was a cop with a duty to protect the integrity of both the crime scene and the investigation. Even so, he couldn't help but acknowledge the woman's authority. Rather than doing his job and ordering her away, he simply nodded. There was so much deference in the gesture that I more than half wondered if the old bat had been his Sunday school teacher once upon a time.

"Austin's mother, Mona, is a good friend of mine," Mayor Kirkpatrick continued. "He's been staying with her ever since his last divorce and becoming more despondent every day. She called me earlier this morning, worried that he had stormed out of the house in such a state that he might do something to harm himself or others."

"Nice of you to let us know," Mel muttered under her breath.

Another vehicle pulled into the lot—a media van. As people sprang out, expecting to set up their equipment, Mayor Kirkpatrick immediately shooed them away. "No cameras and no microphones," she announced firmly before any of the media folk could unpack. "We're dealing with a mental-health issue, and we're required by law to respect the patient's privacy. Isn't that right, Detective Walsh?"

To my amazement, the reporter scurried back to the van without a single word of objection. When it came to wielding influence, Adelina Kirkpatrick was a marvel. Within moments, the entire press corps beat a hasty retreat.

I looked back at the detective. He was clearly torn— torn between doing the right thing as a professional cop and knowing which side his bread was buttered on; between the old guard, the mayor, and the new guard, Mel; between Manson, a guy he'd come up with through the ranks, and Mel, his new chief. The old guard won hands down.

"Yes, ma'am," Walsh said.

Mel was offended. "A mental-health issue?" she stormed. "Are you kidding me? Is that how you expect to handle all of this? Austin Manson attacked me, kidnapped me, and threatened to kill me, and you expect me to forget about all that and let you sweep it under the rug by saying he suffered some kind of psychotic breakdown? You're engaging in an illegal cover-up and expecting me to go along with it?"

"As I said, Austin's mother and I are best friends," Mayor Kirkpatrick explained. "Mona will see to it that her son gets the best possible treatment. Sending him to jail certainly won't fix it. And in this day and age, when police departments operate under so much suspicion, letting word get out that one of our sworn officers has gone on a potentially murderous rampage isn't going to do your department any favors, and it won't do my administration any good either."

"But . . ." Mel began, but Mayor Kirkpatrick talked right over her, speaking loud enough now for all the officers within earshot to hear what she was saying.

"Chief Soames has just informed me that Assistant Chief Manson was threatening suicide earlier today. She, with the aid of her husband . . ." She stopped and looked at me, pleading for assistance.

"Beaumont," I said helpfully. "J. P. Beaumont. Mel wanted to keep her own name, you see."

Mel jabbed me in the rib with her elbow while Mayor Kirkpatrick continued on her merry way.

"She and Mr. Beaumont here have just now managed to subdue him. Assistant Chief Manson is about to be transported to a facility where he'll be given the kind of treatment he requires. In the meantime, let's give Chief Soames and Mr. Beaumont a round of applause!"

Enthusiastic clapping echoed through the parking

lot around us. For once in her life, Mel was caught flat-footed and dumbstruck besides. She had been completely outmaneuvered by a politician who had somehow succeeded in turning Mel Soames into a reluctant ally. With Manson gone, maybe the undercurrent of objection to Mel's tenure as chief would be gone as well.

By the time the applause ended, Detective Walsh was nowhere to be seen. The incident had been publicly declared over and done with. Mel was furious, but I, for one, was grateful. Yes, letting it go that way amounted to crappy police work, but I was glad the mayor had stopped the process before the interviews started and before Mel and I had been forced to perjure ourselves. Besides, the whole shebang had turned into a nonevent. No one had died in the incident. No weapons had been discharged. No one was going to jail. It was a done deal.

The tour bus left shortly after the ambulance departed. Before the bus drove away, I jotted down Sam's name and address so I could send him his promised carton of cigarettes. I didn't mention to Mel I had been forced to smoke a cigarette in my effort to save her life. Since she herself was a relatively recent ex-smoker, she most likely would have thought I volunteered.

Half an hour later, Mel and I left the now-empty parking lot where, as far as the rest of the world was concerned, nothing at all had happened. We went back to the house on Bayside. We stopped by Mel's car long enough to collect her missing purse, phone, and shoe. The other black pump had turned up in the trunk of Manson's Malibu, as well as Mel's backup weapon.

With Mel properly shod again, we went around to the front of the house, stripped off the crime-scene tape, and went inside. Mel took advantage of the relative privacy of our expansive wallboard-free living room to peel off her tattered panty hose. When we left the house again, after closing and locking the front door, Mel tossed the remains of her panty hose on top of a pile of construction debris in the Dumpster parked next to her Porsche.

Then, driving two cars, we headed into Fairhaven, found parking places on the main drag, and were shown to a quiet corner table in Dirty Dan Harris's, a small bistro that has the reputation of being the best restaurant in town.

We placed our order for an early dinner and sat there holding hands across the white-linen tablecloth. We both knew how close we'd come to losing it all that day, and we were very grateful.

"This isn't over," Mel said determinedly. "I should have Walsh's ears for this."

"It'll be better for you if you don't," I advised. "With the mayor all over him, the man was caught between a rock and hard place. He knows he was in the wrong. In terms of having the trust of your rank and file, as well as having his long-term loyalty, resolving it without turning it into a public outcry is a better bet. Without that trust, you're going to end up being a short-timer."

Mel thought about that. "Maybe you're right," she said.

Our food came then, and we tore into it. We had both missed lunch, and we were starving. It wasn't until we were sharing a dessert of bread pudding that things turned serious again.

"Where do we go from here?" Mel asked.

"Well," I said, "I assume that tomorrow morning, you'll go back to being Chief of Police although, for my money, I'd just as soon you refrained from being locked in another car anytime soon."

"What about you?" Mel asked.

"What do you mean what about me? I'm not exactly sitting around letting the grass grow under my steel-belted radials. I'm finishing up Harry's project and will be starting on ours as soon as his is out of the way. I can only handle one housing crisis at a time. I'm sure Jim Hunt will be dragging me hither and yon looking at plumbing fixtures, slab samples, and lighting options."

"That may be what we need you to be doing right now," Mel allowed, "but I don't see much of a future in it. You don't plan on spending the rest of your life supervising construction projects, do you?"

"No," I admitted. "It's something I can do in a pinch if I have to, but you're right. It's not really me."

"There you go," Mel said, nodding, leaning back in her chair and giving me one of those questioning, raised-eyebrow, Mr.-Spock looks that I find so endearing. "So what are you going to do with the rest of your life?"

It was a serious question—one I had been dodging for months—so I did my best to laugh it off. "Bowling, maybe?" I asked. "Or what about golf? Golf seems to be working just fine for Ralph Ames."

Ralph came into my life about the time my second wife, Anne Corley, shot through my world like a speeding comet and transformed my existence. Ralph was Anne's attorney to begin with and became mine in the aftermath of her death. We've had a client/friend relationship for decades, one that continues even now that he's semiretired. Mel leaned forward in her seat and gave me one of her most beguiling smiles. I knew at once that I'd stepped into a trap although it hadn't yet sprung shut.

"I'm so glad to hear you mention Ralph," Mel said. "What about TLC?"

TLC, aka The Last Chance, is Ralph's baby, the same way S.H.I.T. once belonged to Ross Connors. It started years ago when one of Ralph's already well-heeled clients, a woman named Hedda Brinker, hit a huge Powerball jackpot. Hedda's daughter, Ursula had been murdered years earlier, and at the time the crime was as yet unsolved. Hedda wanted to use her jackpot winnings to start a privately operated cold-case organization. Hedda's original vision was that Ralph, operating in the capacity of her attorney, would set things in motion and then step away. Instead, he had remained at the helm.

After the shuttering of Special Homicide, Ralph had suggested that I should maybe think about joining up with TLC. Every time he mentioned it, I had turned him down. Unfortunately, my last cold-case experience had been an ill-fated effort that had resulted in the death of Seattle Homicide Detective Delilah Ainsworth. I knew too well how otherwise good intentions could have fatal consequences. Only three people knew how much Delilah's death had rocked my world— Mel; my AA sponsor and former step-grandfather, Lars Jensen; and Ralph Ames.

As far as I was concerned, I was out of the homicide business, especially when it came to cold cases.

"Being a homicide cop is in your blood," Mel insisted. "Just look at what you did today. You were back in your element out there and saved my life in the process. You're a savvy guy, mister. You know what you're about, you've still got the moves, and I know TLC would be lucky to have you."

"What are you saying then?" I asked. "No bowling and no golf?"

We both laughed at the very idea. Laughter came easily that evening, and it's no wonder.

"Yes," she agreed, "no to both, so are you going to call Ralph about this, or should I?"

It was the old Fuller Brush assumed-close routine all over again—How do you want to pay for this, cash or check?

"Let me think about it," I said. "Give it a little time. Let me get this housing stuff under control, then I'll give Ralph a call."

"Promise?" Mel asked.

"I promise," I said.

And just like that, I knew I was toast. I also knew that TLC was definitely in my future because Mel was right. Over-the-hill or not, being a cop isn't only what I do. Like it or lump it, it's who I am.

Years ago, Amos Warren, a prospector, was gunned down out in the desert, and Sheriff Brandon Walker made the arrest in the case. Now, the retired Walker is called in when the alleged killer, John Lassiter, refuses to accept a plea deal that would release him from prison with time served. Lassiter wants Brandon and The Last Chance to find Amos's "real" killer and clear his name.

Sixteen hundred miles to the north in Seattle, J. P. Beaumont is at loose ends after the Special Homicide Investigation Team, affectionately known as S.H.I.T., has been unexpectedly and completely disbanded. When Brandon discovers that there are links between Lassiter's case and an unsolved case in Seattle, he comes to Beau for help.

Those two cases suddenly become hot when two young boys from the reservation, one of them with close ties to the Walker family, go missing. Can two seasoned cops, working together, decipher the missing pieces in time to keep them alive?

Keep reading for an exciting sneak peek
at J. A. Jance's upcoming novel

Dance of the Bones

A Beaumont and Walker Novel

Coming soon in hardcover from William Morrow

Amos Warren walked with his shoulders stooped and his eyes and mind focused on the uneven ground beneath his feet. The winter rains had been more than generous this year, and this part of the Sonoran desert, Soza Canyon on the far eastern edge of the Rincon Mountains, was alive with flowers. Scrawny, suntanned, and weathered, Amos was more than middle-aged and still remarkably fit. Even so, the sixty or seventy pounds he carried in the sturdy pack on his shoulders weighed him down and had him feeling his sixty-plus years.

He had started the day by picking up several top-notch arrowheads. He slipped several of them into the pockets of his jeans rather than risk damaging them as the load in the pack increased over the course of the day. The one he considered to be the best of the lot, he hid away inside his wallet, congratulating himself on the fact that his day was off to such a great start. In the course of the morning, he located several geodes. The best of those was a bowling-ball-sized treasure that would fetch a pretty penny once it joined the growing collection of goods that he and his foster son, John Lassiter, would offer for sale at the next available gem and mineral show.

Assuming, of course, that John ever spoke to him

again, Amos thought ruefully. The knock-down, drag-out fight the two men had gotten into the night before had been a doozy, and recalling it had cast a pall over Amos's entire day. He had known John Lassiter for decades, and this was the first time he had ever raised a hand to the younger man. The fact that they had duked it out over a girl, of all things, only added to Amos's chagrin.

Ava Martin, Amos thought, what a conniving little whore! She was good-looking and knew it. She was a tiny-blond-bombshell type with just the right curves where they counted. Amos didn't trust the bitch any further than he could throw her.

His next thought was all about John. The poor guy was crazy about Ava—absolutely crazy. As far as John was concerned, Ava was the greatest thing since sliced bread. In fact, he was even talking about buying an engagement ring, for God's sake!

As for Amos? He knew exactly who Ava was and what she was all about. She wasn't anything close to decent marriage material. He had noticed the wicked little two-timer batting her eyes and flirting with John's best friend, Ken—all behind John's back, of course. And two days ago, when John had been out of town, she'd gone so far as to come by his house—forty-five minutes from town—where she had tried putting the moves on Amos.

That was the last straw. Amos was decades older than Ava. He had no illusions about his actually being physically attractive to her. No, she wasn't looking to get laid; Ava was after the main chance.

She knew John and Amos were partners who split everything fifty-fifty. She probably understood that, for the most part, Amos was the brains of the outfit while John was the brawn. Amos was the one who knew where to go searching and find the hidden treasures the unyielding desert would reveal to only the most patient of searchers. He knew what was worth taking home and what wasn't. John was the packhorse who carried the stuff and loaded it into the back of the truck and carried it into the storage unit.

When it came to selling their finds, Amos had years' worth of contacts at his disposal, all of them listed in his little black book. He had collected a whole catalogue of gem and mineral dealers and artifact dealers, some aboveboard and others not so much. He also knew which items might interest individual dealers. He did the behind-the-scenes selling while John handled direct sales at booths in the various venues. John was a good-looking young hunk, and that was always a good thing when it came to face-to-face sales.

Amos suspected that John had gotten into his cups and talked too much about what they did and how much money they brought in—something Amos regarded as nobody's business but their own. He was convinced that was what Ava Martin was really after—the shortest route to the money. Amos had sent the little witch packing, and he'd had no intention of telling John about it, but Ava had gotten the drop on him. She had told John all about their little set-to. The problem was, in Ava's version of the story, Amos had been the one putting the make on her. With predictable results.

The previous evening, Amos had gone to El Barrio, a run-down bar on Speedway just east of I-10. When he'd lived in town, El Barrio had been within walking distance of the house. When developers came through and bought up the whole block where his house was, Amos had taken his wad of money and paid cash for a five-acre place up in Golder Canyon, on the far back side of Catalina. The house was a tin-roofed affair that had started out long ago as a stage stop. In town, John and Amos had been roommates. The "cabin," as Amos liked to call it, was strictly a one-man show, so John had chosen to stay on in town—closer to the action—and had rented a place in the old neighborhood.

When Amos went to El Barrio that night, he had done so deliberately, knowing it was most likely still John's favorite hangout. And knowing, too, that he was coming there to have it out with John because Amos had made up his mind. Either Ava went or John did. He'd been sitting at the bar, tucked in among the other twenty or so Happy Hour regulars and sipping his way through that evening's boilermaker, when John had stormed in through the front door.

"You bastard!" the younger man muttered under his breath as he slid uninvited onto an empty stool next to Amos.

Amos knew that John was hot-tempered, and he was clearly spoiling for a fight—something Amos preferred to avoid. He had come here hoping to talk things out rather than duking them out.

He took a careful sip of his drink. "Good afternoon to you, too," he responded calmly. "Care for a beer?"

"I don't want a beer from you. Or anything else, either. You keep telling me that Ava's bad news, telling me she's not good enough for me, but the first time my back is turned, you try getting her into the sack!"

"That what Ava told you?" Amos asked.

"It's not just what she told me," John declared, his voice rising. "It's what happened."

"What if I told you Ava was a liar?"

"In that case, how about we step outside so I can beat the crap out of you?"

Looking in the mirror behind the bar, Amos saw the reflection of John as he was now—a beefy man four inches taller than Amos, thirty pounds heavier, and three decades younger with a well-deserved reputation as a brawler and an equally well deserved moniker, Big Bad John. Amos's problem was that, at the same time he saw that image, he was remembering another one as well—one of a much younger kid, freckle-faced and missing his two front teeth. That was how John—Johnny back then—had looked when Amos had first laid eyes on him.

Amos knew that in a fair fight between them, outside the bar, he wouldn't stand a chance; he'd be dog meat. The younger man might not have been tougher, but he was younger and taller. By the time a fight was over, most likely the cops would be called. One or the other of them, or maybe both, would be hauled off to jail and charged with assault. Amos had already done time, and he didn't want anything like that to happen to John. That in a nut-shell took the fair-fight option off the table. What Amos needed was a one-, two-punch effort that put a stop to the whole affair before it had a chance to get started.

As the quarrel escalated, tension crept like a thick fog throughout the room, and the rest of the bar went dead quiet.

"I don't want to fight you, kid," Amos said in a con-ciliatory tone while calmly pushing his stool away from the bar. No one noticed how he carefully slipped his right hand into the hip pocket of his worn jeans, and no one saw the same hand ease back out into the open again with something clenched in his fist. "Come on, son" he added. "Take a load off, sit down, and have a beer."

"I am not your son!" John growled as he started to get to his feet. "I never was, and I'm not having a beer with you, either, you son of a bitch. We're done, Amos. It's over. Get some other poor stooge to be your partner."

Big Bad John Lassiter never saw the punch coming. Amos's powerful right hook caught him unawares and unprepared. His blow broke John's cheekbone and sent him reeling backward, dropping like a rock on the sawdust-covered floor. Big John landed, bloodied face up and knocked cold. In the shocked silence that followed, with all eyes focused on John, no one in the room noticed when Amos Warren slipped the brass knuckles back into his pocket. No, it hadn't been a fair fight, but at least it was over without any danger of its turning into a full-scale brawl.

As John started coming to and tried to sit up, several

people hurried to help him. Amos turned back to the bartender. "No need to call the cops," Amos said. "Next round's on me."

As far as the bartender was concerned, that was good news. He didn't want any trouble, either. "Right," he said, nodding in agreement. "Coming right up."

It took several people to get John back on his feet and work-wise. Someone handed him a bar napkin to help stem the flow of blood that was still pouring from the cut on his cheek, but the wad of paper didn't do much good. The damage was done. His shirt was already a bloody mess.

"See you tomorrow then?" Amos called after John, watching him in the mirror as he staggered unsteadily toward the door.

"Go piss up a rope, Amos Warren," John muttered in reply. "I'll see you in hell first."

That was the last thing John had said to him—I'll see you in hell. They'd quarreled before over the years, most recently several times about Ava, but this was the first time they'd ever come to blows. In past instances, a few days after the dustup, one or the other of them would get around to apologizing, and that would be the end of it. Amos hoped the same thing would happen this time around although, with Ava standing on the sidelines fanning the flames, it might not be that easy to patch things up.

Lost in thought, Amos had been walking generally westward, following the course of the dry creek bed at the bottom of the canyon, some of it sandy and some littered with boulders. During monsoon season, flash floods carrying boulders, tree trunks, and all kinds of other debris would roar downstream. As the water level subsided, and the sand settled out, there was no telling what would be left behind. In the course of the day, Amos had seen plenty of evidence—spoor, hoofprints and paw prints that indicated the presence of wildlife—deer, javelina, and even what Amos assumed to be a black bear. But there was no indication of any human incursions.

At a point where the walls of canyon narrowed precipitously, Amos was forced off the bank and into the creek bed itself. And that was when he saw it—a small hunk of reddish-brown pottery sticking up out of the sand. Dropping his heavy back with a thud, he removed the prospector's pick he carried on his belt and knelt on the sand.

It took several minutes of careful digging to unearth the treasure. Much to his amazement, it was still in one piece. How it could have been washed down the streambed and deposited on a sandy strand of high ground without being smashed to bits was one of the wonders of the universe. Amos suspected that the sand-infused water of a flash flood had buoyed it up before the water had drained out of the sand, leaving the pot on solid ground.

Once it was free of the sand, Amos pulled out his reading glasses and then held the piece close enough to examine it. He realized at once that it was far too small to be a cooking pot. Then he noticed that a faded design of some kind had been etched into the red clay before the pot was fired. A more detailed examination revealed the image of what appeared to be an owl perched on top of a tortoise. The presence of the decorative etching on the pot, along with its size, meant that the piece was most likely ceremonial in nature.

Still holding the tiny but perfect pot in his hands, Amos leaned back on his heels and considered the pot's possible origins. He wasn't someone who had a degree in anthropology, but he had spent a lifetime finding and selling Native American artifacts from all over vast stretches of Arizona deserts.

Years of experience told him the pot was most likely Papago in origin. Sometimes known as the Tohono O'Odham, the Papagos had lived for thousands of years in the vast deserts surrounding what was now Tucson. This particular spot, on the far southeastern flanks of the Rincon Mountains, overlooked the San Pedro Valley. It was on the easternmost edge of the Papagos' traditional territory and deep into the part of the world once controlled and dominated by the Apache. Had a stray band of Tohono O'odham come here to camp or hunt and left this treasure behind? Amos wondered. More likely, the tiny artifact had been a trophy of some kind, spoils of war carried off by a marauding band of Apache.

Since the pot had clearly been washed downstream, there was a possibility that a relatively undisturbed site was sitting undiscovered farther up the canyon. There were several professors at the U of A who would pay Amos good money as a finder's fee, so they could go in and do a properly documented excavation. As to the pot itself? Regardless of where it was from, Amos knew he had found a remarkable piece, one that was inherently valuable. The curators at the Heard Museum would jump at having a whole undamaged pot like that for their Southwestern collection. Amos knew that most of the pots on display in the museum had been pieced back together, and there was a reason for that.

The Tohono O'odham believed that the pot maker's spirit remained trapped inside the pots. As a consequence, when the pot maker died, tradition demanded that all her pots be smashed to pieces. So why was this one still whole? That made the idea of its being stolen goods much more likely. The Apache would have no reason to follow Tohono O'odham customs. Why free a dead enemy's spirit. What good would that do for you?

Wanting to protect his treasure, Amos put the pot down and then tore a strip of material from the tail of his ragged, flannel work shirt. The material was old and thin enough that it gave way without a struggle. He wrapped the pot in the strip of material. Then, stowing the protected pot as the topmost item in his bag, he shouldered his load and headed back to the truck. It was early afternoon, but he wanted to be back over Redington Pass early enough that the setting sun wouldn't be directly in his eyes.

Making his way back down the streambed, he kept a close watch on his footing, avoiding loose rocks wherever possible. With the heavily laden pack on his back, even a small fall might result in a twisted ankle or a broken bone, and one of those could be serious business when he was out here all by himself with no way of letting anyone know exactly where he was and no way of summoning help. And rocks weren't the only danger.

On this late-spring afternoon, rattlesnakes emerging from hibernation were out in force. In fact, halfway back to his truck, a diamondback, almost invisible on the sandy surroundings, slithered past him when he stopped long enough to wipe away the sweat that was running into his eyes. That pause had been a stroke of luck for both Amos and the snake. If left undisturbed, snakes didn't bother him. Most of the time, they went their way while Amos went his. But if he'd stepped on the creature unawares, all bets would have been off. One way or the other, the snake would have been dead and even, in spite of his heavy hiking boots, Amos might well have been badly bitten in the process.

Amos's lifetime search for gemstones, minerals, fossils, and artifacts had put him in mountains like this for decades. Watching the snake slide silently and safely off into the sparse underbrush served as a reminder that snakes, javelinas, bobcats, deer, and even black bear had been the original inhabitants of this still-untamed place. Humans, including both the Tohono O'odham and the Apache who had roamed these arid lands for thousands of years, were relative, and probably somewhat unwelcome, intruders. White men, including Amos himself, were definitely Johnny-come-latelies in this solitary place.

Reshouldering his pack, Amos allowed as how he was missing John's presence about then. These days, he was finding it harder to go back downhill than it was to climb up. And with the weight in the pack? Well, he would have appreciated having someone to carry half the load. John might have said they were quits, but as far as Amos was concerned, they were still partners, and they would split everything fifty-fifty.

And there he was doing it again—thinking about John. An hour or so after the altercation, when Amos had left the bar, he might have looked as though he hadn't a care in the world, but he did. His heart was heavy. He might have won the battle, but he was worried he had lost the war.

Despite the fact that they weren't blood relations, they were peas in a pod. Hot-tempered? Check. Too fast with the fists? Check. Didn't care to listen to reason? Check. Thirty years earlier, Amos had hooked up with a girl named Hattie Smith, who had been the same kind of bad news for him as Ava was for John. A barroom fight over Hattie the evening of Amos's twenty-first birthday had resulted in an involuntary manslaughter charge that had sent Amos to the slammer for five to ten. He recognized that there was a lot of the old pot-and-kettle routine here.

Yes, Amos had gotten his head screwed on straight in the course of those six years. He had read his way through a tattered copy of the *Encyclopedia Britannica* that he found in the prison library, giving himself an education that would have compared favorably to any number of college degrees. Even so, he didn't want John to go through the same school of hard knocks. He wanted to protect the younger man from all that because John Lassiter was the closest thing to a son Amos Warren would ever have.

John had grown up next door to Amos's family home. They had lived in a pair of dilapidated but matching houses on a dirt street on Tucson's far west side. Amos lived there because he had inherited the house from his mother. Once out of prison, he had neither the means nor the ambition to go looking for something better. John's family rented the place next door because it was cheap, and cheap was the best they could do.

To Amos's way of thinking, John's parents had been little more than pond scum. His father was a drunk. His mother was a whore who regularly locked the poor kid outside in the afternoons while she entertained her various gentleman callers. On one especially rainy, winter's day, Amos had been outraged to see John, sitting on the front porch, shivering in the cold. He'd been shoved outside in his bare feet and a ragged pair of pajamas.

Amos had ventured out in the yard and stood on the far side of the low rock wall that separated them. "What're you doing?" Amos had asked.

"Waiting," came the disconsolate answer. "My mom's busy."

For months, Amos had seen the cars coming and going in the afternoons while old man Lassiter wasn't at home. Amos had understood all too well what was really going on. He also knew what it was like to be locked out of the house. Back when he was a kid, the same thing had happened to him time and again. In his case, it had been so Amos's father could beat the crap out of Amos's mother in relative peace and quiet. What was going on in the Lassiter household might have been a slightly different take on the matter, but it was close enough.

Without a word, Amos had gone back inside. When he reappeared, he came back to the fence armed with a peanut butter and jelly sandwich.

"Hungry?" he asked.

Without further prompting, the boy had scampered barefoot across the muddy yard. Grabbing the sandwich, he gobbled it down.

"My name's Amos. What's yours?"

"John," the boy mumbled through a mouthful of peanut butter.

"Have you ever played Chinese checkers?"

John shook his head. "What's Chinese checkers?"

"Come on," Amos said. "I'll teach you."

He had hefted the kid up over the wall, shifted him onto his hip, and carried him to his own house. That had been their beginning. Had Amos Warren been some kind of pervert, it could have been the beginning of something very bad, but it wasn't. Throughout John's chaotic childhood, Amos Warren had been the only fixed point in the poor kid's life, his only constant. John Lassiter, Sr., died in a drunk-driving one-car rollover when his son was in fourth grade. By the time John was in high school, his mother, Sandra, had been through three more husbands, each one being a step worse than the one preceding.

Despite John's mother's singular lack of mothering and because he ate more meals at Amos's house than he did at home, John had grown like crazy. More than six feet tall by the time he was in seventh grade, John would have been a welcome addition to any junior-high or high-school athletic program, but Sandra had insisted that she didn't believe in "team sports." What she really didn't believe in was going to the trouble of getting him signed up, paying for physicals or uniforms, or going to and from games or practices. Amos suspected that she didn't want John involved in anything that might have interfered with her barfly social life and late-afternoon assignations, which were now conducted somewhere away from home, leaving John on his own night after night.

Amos knew that the good kids were the ones who were involved in constructive activities after school. The bad kids were left to their own devices. It came as no surprise to Amos that John ended up socializing with the baddies. By the time he hit high school, he had too much time on his hands and a bunch of badass friends.

As a kid, Amos had earned money for Saturday afternoon matinees in downtown Tucson by scouring the roadsides and local teenager party spots for discarded pop bottles, which he had turned over to Mr. Yee, the old man who ran the tiny grocery store on the corner. When Amos happened to come across some pieces of broken Indian pottery, Mr. Yee had been happy to take those off his hands, too, along with Amos's first-ever arrowhead. From then on, the old Chinaman had been willing to buy whatever else Amos was able to scrounge up.

Once Amos got out of prison, he discovered there weren't many employment options available for paroled felons. As a result, he had returned to his onetime hobby of scouring his surroundings for treasures. He knew the desert flatlands like he knew the backs of his own hands, and he knew the mountains as well, the rugged ranges that marched across the lower landscape like so many towering chess pieces scattered across the desert floor—the Rincons and the Catalinas, the Tortolitas and the Huachucas, the Pelloncios and the Chiricahuas.

Now, though, with the benefit of Amos's store of prison-gained knowledge, he was far more educated about what he found. He was able to locate plenty of takers for those items without the need for someone like Mr. Yee to act as a middleman. He earned a decent if modest living and was content with his solitary life. Then John Lassiter got sent to juvie. Amos, claiming to be the kid's most recent stepfather, was the one who had bailed him out and took him home. From then on, that's where John had lived—in the extra room at Amos's house rather than next door with his mother.

By then, Amos could see that the die was cast. John wasn't going to go to college. If he was ever going to amount to anything, Amos would have to show him how to make that happen. From then on, Amos set out to teach John what he knew. Every weekend and during the long, broiling summers, John went along with Amos on those long desert scavenger hunts. Most of the time, John made himself useful by carrying whatever Amos found. Nevertheless, he was an apt pupil. Over time, he became almost as good at finding stuff as Amos was, and between them, their unofficial partnership made a reasonably good living.

Not wanting to attract attention to any of his special hunting grounds, Amos usually parked his jeep a mile at least from any intended target. This time, he had left the vehicle hidden in a grove of mesquite well outside the mouth of the canyon. Approaching the spot where he'd left the truck, Amos caught a tiny whiff of cigarette smoke floating in the air.

John was a chain smoker—something else the two of them argued about constantly, bickering like an old married couple. This time, however, Amos's spirits lifted slightly as soon as his nostrils caught wind of the smoke. This out-of-the-way spot was a place he and John visited often. Maybe the kid had come to his senses after all and followed him here. Maybe it was time to apologize and let bygones be bygones, and if John wanted Ava Martin in his life, so be it.

Once inside the grove, Amos looked around and saw no sign of John or his vehicle, either. That was hardly surprising. Maybe he had chosen some other place to park. There was always a chance John had gone out to do some scavenging of his own.

Amos turned his attention to the pack, unshouldering it carefully and settling it into the bed of the truck. Reaching inside the pack, his fingers located the wadded-up shirt. Feeling through the fabric, he was relieved to find that the pot was still in one piece.

A new puff of smoke wafted past him. That was when he sensed something else, something incongruous underlying the smell of burning cigarette—a hint of perfume. He turned and was dismayed to see Ava standing a mere five feet away. She was holding a weapon that Amos reckoned to be a .22 revolver, probably the very one he had given John for his birthday several months earlier.

"What are you doing here?" he demanded. "Where's John?"

"Don't move," she warned. "I know how to use this thing."

"Where's John?" Amos repeated.

"He's not here?"

"Why are you? How did you know to come here?"

"John and I have been here together several times. You know, for picnics and such. He told me this was where you'd be today."

Outrage boiled in Amos's heart. John had brought her here? He'd shown her this very special hunting ground, one Amos had shared with no one else but John?

The depth of her betrayal was breathtaking. Amos took a step forward. "Why, you little bitch . . ." he began. He never had a chance to finish his threat.

Ava had told him the truth. She really did know how to use the weapon in her hand. Her first bullet caught him clean in the heart. Amos Warren was dead before he hit the ground. The second and third bullets—the unnecessary ones? Those she fired just for good measure—simply because she could. And those were what the prosecutor would later label as overkill and a sign of rage when it came time to try John Lassiter for first-degree murder.

About the Author

J. A. JANCE is the *New York Times* bestselling author of the J. P. Beaumont series, the Joanna Brady series, the Ali Reynolds series, and four interrelated thrillers about the Walker Family as well as a volume of poetry. Born in South Dakota and brought up in Bisbee, Arizona, Jance lives with her husband in Seattle, Washington, and Tucson, Arizona.

Discover great authors, exclusive offers, and more at hc.com.